HELLO, I'm THEA!

I'm *Geronimo Stilton*'s sister. As I'm sure you know from my brother's bestselling novels, I'm a special correspondent for *The Rodent's Gazette*, Mouse Island's most famous newspaper. Unlike my 'fraidy mouse brother, I absolutely adore traveling, having adventures, and meeting rodents from all around the world!

The adventure I want to tell you about begins at Mouseford Academy, the school I went to when I was a young mouseling. I had such a great experience there as a student that I came back to teach a journalism class.

When I returned as a grown mouse, I met five really special students: Colette, Nicky, Pamela, Paulina, and Violet. You could hardly imagine five more different mouselings, but they became great friends right away. And they liked me so much that they decided to name their group after me: the Thea Sisters! I was so touched by that, I decided to write about their adventures. So turn the page to read a fabumouse adventure about the

THEA SISTERS!

Name: Nicky
Nickname: Nic
Home: Australia
Secret ambition: Wants to be an ecologist.
Loves: Open spaces and nature.
Strengths: She is always in a good mood, as long as she's outdoors!
Weaknesses: She can't sit still!
Secret: Nicky is claustrophobic — she can't stand being in small, tight places.

niCkY

Nicky

COLETTE

Name: Colette

Nickname: It's Colette, please. (She can't stand nicknames.)

Home: France

Secret ambition: Colette is very particular about her appearance. She wants to be a fashion writer.

Loves: The color pink.

Strengths: She's energetic and full of great ideas.

Weaknesses: She's always late!

Secret: To relax, there's nothing Colette likes more than a manicure and pedicure.

Colette

VIOLET

Name: Violet
Nickname: Vi
Home: China
Secret ambition: Wants to become a great violinist.
Loves: Books! She is a real intellectual, just like my brother, Geronimo.
Strengths: She's detail-oriented and always open to new things.
Weaknesses: She is a bit sensitive and can't stand being teased. And if she doesn't get enough sleep, she can be a real grouch!
Secret: She likes to unwind by listening to classical music and drinking green tea.

Violet

Name: Paulina

Nickname: Polly

Home: Peru

Secret ambition: Wants to be a scientist.

Loves: Traveling and meeting people from all over the world. She is also very close to her sister, Maria.

Strengths: Loves helping other rodents.

Weaknesses: She's shy and can be a bit clumsy.

Secret: She is a computer genius!

PAULINA

PAULINA

Name: Pamela

Nickname: Pam

Home: Tanzania

Secret ambition: Wants to become a sports journalist or a car mechanic.

Loves: Pizza, pizza, and more pizza! She'd eat pizza for breakfast if she could.

Strengths: She is a peacemaker. She can't stand arguments.

Weaknesses: She is very impulsive.

Secret: Give her a screwdriver and any mechanical problem will be solved!

Pamela

Geronimo Stilton

Thea Stilton
AND THE SPANISH DANCE MISSION

Scholastic Inc.

ISBN 978-0-545-55626-2

Copyright © 2012 by Edizioni Piemme S.p.A., Corso Como 15, 20154 Milan, Italy.

International Rights © Atlantyca S.p.A.

English translation © 2013 by Atlantyca S.p.A.

Based on an original idea by Elisabetta Dami.

www.geronimostilton.com

Published by Scholastic Inc., 557 Broadway, New York, NY 10012. SCHOLASTIC and associated logos are trademarks and/or registered trademarks of Scholastic Inc.

Stilton is the name of a famous English cheese. It is a registered trademark of the Stilton Cheese Makers' Association. For more information, go to www.stiltoncheese.com.

Text by Thea Stilton
Original title *Missione "flamenco"*
Cover by Giuseppe Facciotto
Illustrations by Chiara Balleello (design) and Daniele Verzini (color)
Graphics by Chiara Cebraro

Special thanks to Beth Dunfey
Translated by Emily Clement
Interior design by Kay Petronio

12 11 10 9 8 7 6   14 15 16 17 18/0

Printed in the U.S.A.   40
First printing, September 2013

A MUSICAL SURPRISE

I was SCURRYING home after interviewing my local theater's artistic director. He had **PROUDLY** announced that they would be starting their season with a program of traditional dances from all over the world!

I couldn't wait to tell the Thea Sisters! Just a few months ago, they had taken part in a **workshop** on traditional dance.

Oh, pardon me, I almost forgot to introduce myself. My name is Thea Stilton,

and I am a special correspondent for *The Rodent's Gazette,* Mouse Island's biggest newspaper. A little while back, I taught a class in **ADVENTURE** journalism at **MOUSEFORD ACADEMY**. Colette, Nicky, Pamela, Paulina, and Violet — the THEA SISTERS — were my star students.

As I entered my house, I noticed my friends had sent me a package. It contained a **CD** and a note:

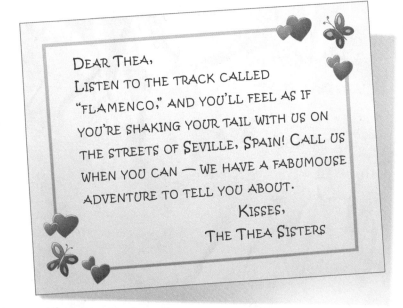

DEAR THEA,
LISTEN TO THE TRACK CALLED "FLAMENCO," AND YOU'LL FEEL AS IF YOU'RE SHAKING YOUR TAIL WITH US ON THE STREETS OF SEVILLE, SPAIN! CALL US WHEN YOU CAN — WE HAVE A FABUMOUSE ADVENTURE TO TELL YOU ABOUT.

KISSES,
THE THEA SISTERS

In the blink of a cat's eye, I'd inserted the disc into my laptop. A moment later, the distinctive sound of flamenco, a style of music and dance that is popular in Spain, FLOATED into my living room.

I immediately called the Thea Sisters to thank them — and to get the scoop on their new adventure. It was sure to be action-packed!

ON VACATION...
AT SCHOOL!

Colette **whirled** into Paulina's room like a pink tornado. She dropped her backpack, which was **bursting** with papers and notes, and collapsed into an armchair. "Thank goodmouse I'm done at last. Professor Marblemouse's final exam was **harder** than a block of aged cheddar!"

"Congrats, sis!" exclaimed Nicky, passing her friend a Swiss smoothie. "I hope you're ready to relax, because our two weeks of vacation begin now! ALL that's left is to figure out what we want to do."

"How about a nice

trip to Greece?" asked Violet, looking up from a TRAVEL brochure. "There are so many amazing archeological sites there. . . ."

"Patagonia would be great, too. Look at these gorgeous p h o t o s!" said Pam, holding up a magazine.

Paulina's eyes were glued to her laptop's screen. "Beautiful — but I just found a GREAT flight to Honduras. . . ."

"Mouselets, I barely have the ENERGY to run myself a bath!" Colette moaned. "I'm practically falling asleep on my paws! I'm not sure I can even muster the STRENGTH to deep-condition my fur."

The mouselets all STARED at her in disbelief.

"Are you really that tired?" Pam asked at last.

Colette shrugged. "Well, you know I love to make a mountain out of a mousehill. But this term *was* super-challenging. I'm ready for some serious relaxation."

"Actually," Nicky began, "that sounds pretty good to me, too. I wouldn't mind putting my **PAWS UP** for a while . . . maybe hit the beach . . ."

"I'd love to spend every afternoon playing my violin," Violet added.

"I've been wanting to SET UP a blog for student announcements. My friend Shen and I have been talking about it for months, but we **NEVER** find the time to do it!" Paulina put in.

Pam nodded. "You said it, sis. . . . I've been so busy I haven't even rotated the tires on my **JEEP**!"

Colette got to her paws. "Listen, I have an

idea: Why don't we take a vacation somewhere truly **OUT OF THE WAY**?"

"Where did you have in mind?" Paulina asked.

"I'm thinking of a place that we'll all REALLY like . . . someplace comfortable, where it's easy to get around. Someplace we can relax, but also hit the gym if we feel like it. Someplace that's full of friendly rodents . . ."

"All right! When do we leave?" Pam asked enthusiastically.

"We're already there," Colette said, smiling. "It's **MOUSEFORD ACADEMY!**"

Her *friends* stared at her for a moment, then burst out laughing.

"You know, I think *Colette* is onto something," Violet said once the laughter had subsided. "We're always so *busy* that we never get to enjoy the academy and Whale Island!"

"Then it's *decided*: This time, we're staying put," Nicky concluded.

At that moment, there was a knock at the door. "Mouselets! I have a package for you!"

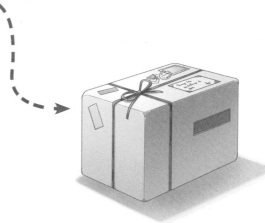

SPAIN, HERE WE COME!

Paulina opened the door. In front of her was an enormouse **box** in the paws of Mercury Whale, the local mailmouse. "Where should I put it?" he **gasped**.

"Here!" Violet and Pam replied, making room for the **HUGE** package.

"There's a *letter*, too," Mercury said. "Now, where did I leave it?" He stuck his snout into his mailbag.

After a moment, he pulled out a **FIERY-RED** envelope. "Here it is!"

The **mouselets** thanked Mercury. Then

Pam eagerly ripped open the envelope. Inside was a notecard decorated with red roses and a message written by paw:

Dearest Thea Sisters,

The fabumouse World Dance Workshop flew by faster than a tabby doing the tango. We miss you!

Fortunately, we've thought of an event that you simply can't miss! But we don't want to ruin the surprise. Open the package and you'll see what we're squeaking about. Meet us in Seville!

With love,
Anita and Joaquin Vega

"The Vegas!" Nicky exclaimed. "Do you remember how much **fun** we had **together** during the **WORLD DANCE** Workshop?"

"Of course!" Violet replied. "I'll never forget the day Anita taught me the first steps of the *flamenco*. . . ."

"And Joaquin taught us our first spin! Those **TWINS** are great teachers," said Pam.

"It's hard to believe we haven't seen them since the workshop ended six months ago!" Colette sighed. "It was so **HARD** to say good-bye!"

"Something tells me we'll see them again soon!" Paulina exclaimed, lifting off the top of the **box**.

Inside there were five **BRIGHTLY COLORED** packages, one for each of

Violet shows off her Japanese dance costume!

Anita fixes Pam's flamenco fur-do!

Colette dances the hula!

Oops . . . Paulina tangos onto Joaquin's paw!

All together for one last picture!

the mouselets. Paulina quickly PAWED them to her friends. That's when she noticed a FLYER at the bottom of the box.

"What does it say?" Colette asked, clutching her pink package.

"It's an invitation for the Feria de Abril, a big festival in **Seville**!"

"Oh yes, I've heard of it," Nicky said. "It happens every year in spring."

"Absolutely FABUMOUSE!" cried Colette. She had just opened her gift. It was a glamorous flamenco dress made of pink silk. The other mouselets hurried to open their parcels. Soon the room was filled with magnificent dresses, each one edged with *lace* and colorful TRIM.

"Mouselets, this is the kind of invitation we just **CAN'T** pass up! It's a once-in-a-lifetime opportunity. Right?" Pam exclaimed.

FERIA DE ABRIL

Feria de Abril is the most important festival in Seville. This week-long celebration offers an explosion of flowers and music, and happens every spring.

The heart of the festival occurs just outside Seville's city center, in Maria Luisa Park. Here, the city's families and businesses build more than a thousand *casetas*, temporary houses in which they dance, sing, and eat together. Fairgoers dress in the splendid traditional clothing of flamenco dancers. The streets stay busy throughout the night, and during the day, you can admire the elegant horse-drawn carriages that pass by. It's a week of pure entertainment, and everyone is invited!

"Right!" her friends responded **together**.

"All right, then, let's move those paws and start packing!" Nicky said.

"spain is waiting!"

WELCOME TO SEVILLE!

Two days later, the Thea Sisters' plane landed at the airport in **Seville**. The runway was sparkling with dazzling sunshine.

"I'd better put on my hat!" Colette said. "I'd hate to get a sunburn."

"Your **Hat**?" Pam replied. "Which one? You must have brought a dozen with you!"

Colette shrugged. "I don't know what you're squeaking about, Pam. I packed Light for this trip. . . ."

"Really? Then that can't be all your luggage coming down the carousel, can it?" teased Pam, glancing at the **SPLASH OF**

PINK headed their way.

Colette rolled her eyes. "Pam, haven't you ever heard the famous French saying 'Style never takes a vacation'?"

"**NOPE!** In New York, we say, 'The less baggage you've got, the farther you'll go'!"

The two friends continued **BICKERING** all the way to the exit, where they were interrupted by an excited SQUEAL. "Thea Sisters, *bienvenidas**!"

* In Spanish, *bienvenidas* means "welcome."

"Anita! Joaquin!" cried Nicky, *running* to meet them.

After a quick round of hugs, Anita and Joaquin introduced their **friends** to the rest of their family — Mama Lucia, Papa Javier, and older brother Rodrigo.

Everyone piled into the **family** van, which sped toward the city center. Through the windows, the Thea Sisters admired the Spanish **countryside**.

"Look at that **RIVER**!" Pam exclaimed.

"That's the Guadalquivir," **JOAQUIN** explained. "It crosses the entire city."

A few minutes later, the van entered the **city** center. It stopped in front of a **Lovely** old building with a sign bearing words painted by paw:

The Vega School
Dance, Music, and Performance

"We're here!" Joaquin exclaimed.

Seville

Seville is the capital of
ANDALUSIA, a region
in southern Spain. The city
sits on the banks of the river
GUADALQUIVIR, where
Christopher Columbus
embarked on his historic trip to
America.

Madrid

Córdoba

ANDALUSIA

Granada

SEVILLE

The city is famous for its architectural beauty,
including GIRALDA, the famous cathedral bell
tower, and ALCÁZAR, the royal palace. But the
best way to experience the spirit of Seville is to walk
along its twisty streets and get lost in the charming
atmosphere.

A FAMILY TRADITION

Colette, Nicky, Pamela, Paulina, and Violet **followed** their friends inside.

"So, you run this dance school?" Violet *wondered*.

"That's right!" Papa Javier responded proudly. "The school has belonged to our family for generations. It's one of the best-known flamenco schools in the **world**!"

"In the Vega family, you learn music and **dance** before you learn to walk," Anita explained.

Her mother nodded. "Every member of the family has their own specialty: My husband teaches the guitar, Rodrigo teaches singing, and the **TWINS** teach dance."

"We have the best **dancer** in the whole

country!" Joaquin declared. "Come on, I'll introduce you."

The Thea Sisters followed him and Anita into a large practice room. Its walls were covered in MIRRORS, all of which showed the reflection of a dancer spinning with the rhythmic grace of the *flamenco*.

"Aunt Julieta!" Anita exclaimed.

The dancer turned, and a **sweet** smile lit up her snout, which was framed by dark fur tied up in a **BUN**.

"Auntie, we'd like to introduce you to our dear friends Colette, Nicky, Pamela, Paulina, and Violet," Joaquin said.

"I've heard $\mathbb{SO}$ $\mathbb{MUCH}$ about you!" Julieta said, shaking their paws.

"Oh, we don't want to interrupt your rehearsal!" said Colette, **embarrassed**.

"No worries, **mouseLets**! I was just practicing a few steps for the *feria*."

"Yes," Anita added, "Julieta is the star of the big $\mathbb{SHOW}$ that we're putting on to celebrate the school's anniversary."

"**Sizzling spark plugs!** Now I understand why you two are such great dancers," Pam exclaimed. "You learned from a master!"

The twins laughed. "You're right, Pam, that's exactly it!" Anita said.

But Julieta shook her snout. "Actually, the only 'master' is **her**!" She pointed to a large

PAINTING hanging in the middle of the wall. It showed a young dancer in a bright flamenco dress with an open **fan** in her hand.

Rosita Vega

"That's Rosita Vega," Julieta **EXPLAINED**, noticing the mouselets' curious looks. "She was the **GREATEST** flamenco dancer of all time, and also our ancestor — she's my **grandmother**!"

"I've **READ** about her," Violet murmured.

Julieta **smiled**. "Rosita was born in Córdoba, but she moved to **Seville** when she was a little mouselet. In addition to being a famouse flamenco **dancer**, she was a marvemouse singer, and toward the end of

ROSITA CONQUERS SPAIN

Big success for Rosita Vega! Her most recent flamenco show has won praise from critics far and wide. Now the artist has turned to writing songs. She is said to be working on a collection of her own music.

her career, she was also a composer. Unfortunately, hardly any of her songs were recorded. . . ."

She was interrupted by the arrival of her older sister. *"Tapas!"* Mama Lucia exclaimed. She was carrying an enormouse **Plateful** of food.

Joaquin grinned. "That's our MAMA'S specialty. She doesn't sing, and she doesn't dance. Instead, she feeds the whole school!"

"You can't live on music alone!" said Mama

Lucia. She placed the DISH on a small table. "What do you say to a nice SNACK out on the patio?"

Pam's keen snout had SMELLED the *tapas* from afar. "I say that's the most delicious idea I've heard all day!"

TAPAS

You can't leave Spain without trying *tapas,* or small portions of many different dishes. Examples of dishes include sheep's milk cheese, vegetable shish kebabs, meatballs, and potato-and-onion omelets.

No one is certain how the tapas tradition started, although many believe that it began as a way to protect sweet drinks from fruit flies by covering the glasses with small plates. *Tapar* means "to cover" or "to cork." Rather than leave the plates empty, restaurants began filling them with the house specialties!

FLOWERS IN
THEIR FUR

Between snacks and stories, the next few hours passed quickly for the mouselets and their friends. When the sky started to turn **PiNK**, Julieta cried, "Oh no, the flowers!"

"What **flowers**?" Colette asked.

"The ones I wear behind my ears! I need fresh **red roses** to place in my **fur**. It's part of my costume for this evening."

"Would you like us to go pick them up from José?" Anita asked.

"Would you really? I'd like to *practice* my dance steps one more time. . . ."

"Of course," Joaquin said. "It's the perfect excuse to **SHOW** our friends the neighborhood."

Pam was reaching for the last piece of

CHEESE as her friends started to follow the Vega twins outside. "Wait for me!" the mouselet mumbled, her mouth still **FULL**.

"Shake a tail, Pam! We only have a few hours until the *feria*. Do you want to spend **all** of them eating?" Colette joked.

Her friend laughed. "When the food is this **GOOD**, can you blame me?"

The group headed toward the city center. "Before we go to José's, we want to show you **Plaza de España**. It's one of the most beautiful spots in all of Seville," Anita said. She led the Thea Sisters into a large, semicircular stone plaza. The mouselets were AWESTRUCK.

A stately old building encircled the plaza. Right in the center of the square, a fountain was gushing water.

The mouselets could have stayed for hours, soaking in the atmosphere. But Anita pulled them gently by the paws. "We can come back here, I promise. But now we've got to get to the florist's before it closes!"

Disappointed, the Thea Sisters peeled their eyes away and followed Anita and Joaquin down a narrow backstreet.

"Did we take a wrong **TURN**?" Colette asked.

"**NO**, this is the right way. Trust me!" Joaquin said, leading them inside an ancient building.

"Wait . . ." Colette began. But before she could **FINISH**, she was surrounded by a cloud of **INTOXICATING** smells. The Vegas and the mouselets had found the flower shop!

"Wow!" Nicky exclaimed, admiring the colorful blossoms that crowded the shop.

"These are the most beautiful flowers I've ever seen," Paulina gasped.

Plaza de España

Finished in 1929, this marvelous square is one of the most striking sites in Seville. The buildings are covered with spectacular enameled tiles and mosaics.

"I'm so glad to hear that," a male squeak replied from behind a **mass** of roses.

"José, I'd like to introduce our **friends** Colette, Nicky, Pamela, Paulina, and Violet. They're here for the *feria*!" Anita said **HAPPILY**.

"Welcome, mouselets! Are you enjoying **Seville**?" José asked.

"Yes!" Paulina replied. "It's a **FUN** city!"

"And so full of color," Pam added.

"Don't forget the music! It's lovely to hear

the **SOUND** of a guitar on every corner," Violet put in.

"And the **fashion** . . . every mouse in Seville is so *chic*," Colette concluded.

The florist smiled at the mouselets. "It's an honor to meet visitors who really appreciate our fine city!"

"José, do you have the **flowers** for my aunt?" Anita asked.

"Of course. Here they are," José said, pawing her a bunch of red roses **WRAPPED** in paper.

Then he turned to the Thea Sisters and looked them over from the tips of their snouts to the tips of their tails. "And, you, do you have your flowers, **mouseLetS?**"

"Well, no . . . that is . . . uh . . ." Paulina stuttered.

Without another word, José disappeared behind a row of vases. A moment later, he emerged with five gorgeous types of flowers.

"A **YELLOW GERBERA** for you," he said, offering the flower to Paulina. "It's a symbol of happiness and good cheer."

José turned to Pam. "For your sunny personality, a **STRIPED CARNATION!**" Next he addressed Violet. "Here is an *elegant camellia* for a refined and sensible soul.

Daisies are for rodents who love nature, and ORCHIDS are perfect for mice with elegance and style!" he concluded, pawing flowers to Nicky and Colette, respectively.

The mouselets were charmed by José's kind gesture. They THANKED him profusely.

Then they said their good-byes.

As they turned to leave, two young MICE came into the flower shop. . . .

THE NAVARROS

Anita and Joaquin **GREETED** the two newcomers politely. "Oh, hi, Lola. Hi, Pedro."

Lola and Pedro put their snouts in the air and marched up to the counter without a squeak.

Anita shook her snout. "**Arrogant** as **ALWAYS**," she whispered as they left the shop.

"Are they FRIENDS of yours?" Colette asked.

"Not exactly," Anita sighed. "Those are the Navarro twins. Their family runs a flamenco school, too, and they never miss an opportunity to compete with us!"

"There's an old FEUD between our families, so Lola and Pedro never even say hello," Joaquin explained.

"That explains why they LOOKED so grumpy," Nicky said.

As they chattered, the mouselets and their friends strolled back to the Vegas' neighborhood.

"The Navarros' school is right over here!" Anita said, leading the Thea Sisters down a side street.

"It doesn't look like things are going too well for them," commented Violet. The front of the building was crumbling, and the

windows were in bad repair.

Joaquin nodded. "Lately, the Navarros have been struggling, and they **bLaMe** our family for snagging all the dance students."

"We've heard that they may have to close. That would be a real **SHAME**," Anita said.

"But if they weren't so **hard** to deal with, they'd have more students," Joaquin said.

"You're right, Joaquin," Anita said. "But then Seville would lose two **excellent** dancers. Pedro and Lola are wonderful!"

"As **WONDERFUL** as your aunt?" Pam asked.

Anita waved her paw dismissively. "Oh, that's like comparing processed cheese puffs with the finest Brie! There's no one like Auntie Julieta."

"Speaking of Aunt Julieta, she's still waiting for her flowers. **LET'S MOVE OUR TAILS!**" Joaquin said.

FERIA DE ABRIL

Back inside the Thea Sisters' **ROOM** at the Vegas' house, it was impossible to **MOVE** a muscle. Every inch of space — chairs, beds, bureaus, and even the floor — was covered with *clothes*, combs, fans, shoes, and ribbons. Colette's makeup bag was so **big** it practically needed a room of its own!

"Thundering cat tails, I just *knew* I'd forget **SOMETHING**!" Colette cried. "I was in such a hurry when I packed. . . ."

"What'd you forget, Coco? Something important?" Nicky asked.

"Yes! My eye mask," Colette replied. "You know, to **depuff** my eyes."

"Oh, wait a minute, is this it?" Violet asked, pulling the THIN mask from the pages of

her guidebook. "Sorry, I was using it as a bookmark!"

Pam shook her head at all of Colette's beauty supplies. Then she turned back to the MIRROR. "Mouselets, I need your help with my fur!" she exclaimed.

Colette, Nicky, Paulina, and Violet turned to look at Pam . . . and burst out laughing.

"You look crazier than a cat caught in a cyclone!" Paulina said as she came over to help. Furpins were sticking out of Pam's head **randomly** in every direction.

After half an hour wrestling with stuck zippers and unruly curls, the mouselets were finally ready for the **FERIA DE ABRIL**.

"Come on, mouselets,

let's roll!" Pam urged them. "Our friends are waiting for us! We can't be late."

Colette led the pack DOWN the stairs. Joaquin was WAITING in the foyer below. He looked elegant in his deep blue dancing costume.

"You look lovely," Joaquin said.

Colette smiled. "Thank you. It's this gorgeous flamenco dress," she said.

"It's time to take the PLUNGE, mouselets!" cried Nicky. "I can't wait to check out the crowd."

"*Vámonos, chicas*!*" said Anita, joining the little group.

Outside, Colette, Nicky, Pamela, Paulina, Violet, Anita, and Joaquin were immediately Swept up in the festive air of the carnival. The whole city was abuzz with excitement.

"We have to cross the river to reach the

---

* "*Vámonos, chicas*" means "Let's go, girls!" in Spanish.

portada," Joaquin explained.

"The what?" Violet asked.

"The entrance to the *feria*! It's an arch that's built every year just for the occasion. At midnight, all the LIGHTS go on, and we don't want to miss the **SHOW**," Anita explained.

The Thea Sisters followed their friends. Soon, they had blended into the crowd. All around them, rodents were laughing and SQUEAKING on their way to the *portada*.

Suddenly, the darkness was filled with a thousand colored lights.

"That's *el alumbrao*, the lighting!" Anita exclaimed. "Now that the LIGHTS are on, the festival can begin!"

THE SEVILLANA

The mouselets and their friends joined the crowd **passing through** the *portada* to enter the heart of the *feria*.

"Look at all the colored lanterns!" Pam exclaimed.

"It's so beautiful!" Violet said. "I feel like we've entered an **enchanted** city."

The sound of lively music drew Colette to a **tent** across the street.

"The tents are *casetas*, built specially for the *feria*," Joaquin told her. "Inside, you eat and drink with your friends, and you can join in the *flamenco* dancing!"

"Can we go in?" Paulina asked.

"Of course! Let's choose the one we LIKE best," said Anita.

The group made their way deeper into the festival. Rodents dressed in FABUMOUSE flamenco costumes were everywhere. All around them, the mouselets could hear the aching melody of the guitar, mixed with the rhythmic beats of the castanets and the dancers' tapping steps.

"What do you think, should we go in here?" suggested Joaquin, pointing at a TENT.

CASETAS

For the Feria de Abril, over a thousand casetas spring up in Seville. They are small houses made of wood, built for the festival. Some have an intimate family feel. Others have a big, lively, party atmosphere.

As they entered, the crowd made ROOM for them. There was joyful noise all around. At the back of the tent, there was a small **STAGE**, and dancers were performing a wild *sevillana**.

"Wow!" Colette exclaimed with **admiration**. "It would be incredible to know how to dance like that. . . ."

Anita took her paw. "Don't be shy — come with me. We'll build on the steps you learned during the World Dance Workshop!"

Colette was nervous, but she let her friend lead her to the stage. After a few minutes, the lively **RHYTHM** of the guitar won her over. As the crowd clapped to the beat of the music, Colette started to dance with Anita.

"Mouselets, check out our little Coco!" Paulina said. "Isn't she FABUMOUSE?"

Joaquin was about to agree when a voice

---

* *Sevillana* is a type of flamenco.

behind him squeaked, "Greasy cat guts, who's that new **dancer**? She doesn't know her *flamenco* from her fandango!"

The Thea Sisters turned to see the **SCORNFUL** snout of Lola Navarro. She and her brother had come in behind them.

"That's a DEAR friend of mine," Joaquin retorted. "She's only studied flamenco for two weeks, and she's **fantastic**!"

"I don't know if *fantastic* is the word I'd use," Pedro sniffed. "But you Vegas have

never truly understood *flamenco*, so I guess I shouldn't be surprised."

At that moment, Colette and Anita scurried back to their friends. Colette's cheeks were **flushed** from the dance. "How was I?" she asked.

"Wonderful!" Joaquin responded, casting an icy look at the Navarros.

"Pedro! Lola! You're here, too," said Anita. "Why don't we get some water and then go *listen* to Rodrigo's concert?"

"Rodrigo's **PERFORMING**?" Violet asked.

Joaquin nodded. "He's going to sing a song that **NO ONE** has ever heard before. It's an original piece by our great-grandmother Rosita!"

"Why have you kept it secret all this time?" Pedro asked SHARPLY. "If *we* had INHERITED the song, it would already be a hit!"

"Rosita didn't want her song to be SHARED," Anita objected.

"Who cares?" Pedro replied. "Our family would never miss a chance to make money just because of some silly promise!"

"Don't get your whiskers in a twist, Pedro," said Lola. "You're wasting your breath. They'll never understand!"

With that, she flounced out of the tent. Her brother followed her.

"I'm the one who doesn't understand," said Violet. "What were they talking about? Why would they have inherited Rosita's unpublished song?"

"Because the Navarros are our COUSINS!" Joaquin explained.

A FAMILY FEUD

The Thea Sisters stared at their friends in **surprise**.

"Pedro and Lola are descendants of Rosita, like us," Anita explained. "Years ago, the two sides of our family argued and grew apart. Since then, the Navarros consider us their **ENEMIES**!"

"But what happened?" Paulina asked.

"After she came to Seville, Rosita married and had **TWO DAUGHTERS**, Beatriz and Blanca," Joaquin put in. "From the time they were mouselings, the two sisters did nothing but **bicker**!"

"That's **SAD**," said Paulina, thinking of her own little sister, Maria. "There's nothing better

than having a sister you **LOVe**!"

"The **disagreements** between Blanca and Beatriz grew as the years passed," Anita went on. "When they each got **MarrieD**, Blanca to our grandfather and Beatriz to Lola and Pedro's **GRANDFATHER**, they founded two rival schools of flamenco."

"Rosita reluctantly **DIVIDED** her inheritance between them," Anita said. "She asked each daughter what she would like. Beatriz chose the family jewelry, and Blanca chose Rosita's

dance **SECRETS** and a special secret song."

"Is that the one we'll **HEAR** tonight?" Colette asked.

"*Sí*," **JOAQUIN** replied. "For the school's **CENTENNIAL**, our family has organized a small show, just for friends and relatives, and Rodrigo will sing the song."

"It will be a SURPRISE for us, too!" Anita said.

"Where will the concert be?" Pam asked.

"In a *caseta*, of course — ours!" Joaquin smiled. "Follow us!"

The seven friends plunged back into the **colorful** crowd. Soon they came to a *caseta* that was surrounded by a small GROUP of rodents. The sound of a guitar was coming from inside.

"THAT'S PAPA!" Anita exclaimed.

Joaquin, Anita, and the mouselets entered just in time to hear Julieta announce, "Friends, what you are about to hear is a real **treasure**!"

TREASURE

Julieta paused and looked out at the audience. The rodents **dearest** to her were all here in the *caseta,* looking up at her eagerly. The **mouse** cleared her throat and continued. "Now I give you Rodrigo, who will perform a song left to us by our *beloved* Rosita."

Rodrigo smiled and took his place at the center of the **STAGE**, next to his father on guitar. The audience members could see the **emotion** on the snouts of both mice.

A moment later, the first notes of Rosita's song **SWELLED**. As Rodrigo began to sing, the audience was swept up in the **MOMENT**.

My treasure is hidden
In a garden of rose.
The way to its heart
Is something no one knows.

My treasure is known only to me.
It can never be taken apart.
Its key commands the wind,
And it stays always near my heart.

My treasure remains hidden.
It does not easily come out.
It waits for the brightest star
To shine down on my snout.

Where are you, my treasure?
Far and wide will I roam,
Though the place where I'll find you
Is close to my home.

As soon as the final notes rang out, the crowd went wild. The Thea Sisters were so moved, their eyes shone with tears.

Julieta took the microphone again. "Thank you, Rodrigo, for that AMAZING performance! I think each of us has a treasure to keep, just as Rosita wrote. And mine is this splendid fan." She held up a precious fan made of EMBROIDERED silk. "I inherited it from her. It represents my passion for flamenco, which makes every day of my life MORE BEAUTIFUL! Who knows what Rosita's treasure may have been. . . ."

At these words, the Navarro twins, who had come to hear the song, EXCHANGED a meaningful look.

Colette noticed. "Those two are acting weirder than a weasel at a wedding. . . ."

she MURMUReD to herself.

Then a new song DISTRACTED her from the Navarros, and she went back to enjoying the **SHOW** with her friends.

 The Navarros had a strange reaction to Julieta's speech . . . but why?

THE FAN'S THEFT

It had been an amazing **EVENING** for the Thea Sisters. All of Seville seemed to be suspended in a **bubble** of happiness. The mouselets and their friends were way too excited to feel **TIRED**.

But when the shadows of night gave way to **morning**, Violet let out a big yawn. "Should we go get some sleep?"

"I have another *idea*," Anita said.

"Another idea?! After all these hours of dancing, I'm beat!" Pam moaned.

"That's too bad, because I know someplace where we can grab a tasty breakfast. . . ." Anita said, shrugging. But she couldn't stifle a little smile.

"Breakfast? Well, why didn't you say so!"

exclaimed Pam, suddenly recovered. Her **friends** BURST out laughing.

"I suggest *chocolate con churros!*" Anita said.

"Hooray!" Pam replied. "Wait . . . chocolate what?"

"*Churros* are sweet fried dough that we eat with a nice cup of hot chocolate," said Joaquin.

That was all the **EXPLANATION** Pam and the mouselets needed to postpone their bedtime. Fifteen minutes later, they were seated at tables in a famous **BAKERY**. As they ate, they admired the decorated carriages that passed by. An elegantly **HARNESSED** horse led each one.

Colette, Nicky, Pamela, Paulina, Violet, Anita, and Joaquin were still sipping their

hot chocolate when an alarmed squeak cried out, "There you are! Thank goodmouse I've **FINALLY** found you!" Rodrigo scurried up to their table.

"Rodrigo? What's wrong?" Anita asked, surprised.

"Have you seen Julieta's FAN?" her brother asked her.

"Yes, she showed it to the audience while you were singing. It's gorgeous. . . ." Colette replied DREAMILY.

"No, you don't understand! I'm asking if you've seen it *since* my performance, because it's disappeared!"

"How is that possible?" Joaquin asked. "Aunt Julieta **NEVER** lets it out of her sight!"

"I know," replied Rodrigo grimly. "Actually, we think it might have been stolen!"

"What? No! That fan is a precious heirloom

from Rosita!" Anita exclaimed.

"Let's go back to the *caseta* to find our aunt," Joaquin said.

Nicky nodded. "We're coming, too. We'll **HELP** you get it back."

Back at the *caseta*, friends and relatives surrounded Julieta. They were FLOODING her with questions.

"Where did you SEE it last?"

"Did you put it down somewhere?"

"Maybe you loaned it to someone?"

The dancer shook her snout. "I never let go of it. It was in my purse, which I left on my chair to go arrange the flowers in my fur. When I came back to my chair, the fan had DISAPPEARED!"

"Maybe it fell. Let's search the *caseta!*" Colette suggested.

"We've already done that," Julieta sighed. "There's no TRACE of it!"

"I saw a suspicious rodent!" José the florist suddenly declared. "I went out to get some air, and when I came back in, I ran into a mouse I'd never seen before. He was wearing a hat pulled down over his snout and a dark scarf. He was clutching a bag, and the handle of a

fan was sticking out!"

"How do you know it was Rosita's fan?" **DEMANDED** Pedro Navarro. He and his sister had suddenly ReTuRNeD to the *caseta*.

"At the time, I hardly noticed it," José replied, "but now that I think about it, I believe the end of the handle was in the shape of a r𝐨se, just like Julieta's!"

"I saw that rodent, too! He was in a big *HURRY,*" added Vanessa, an old friend of Julieta's. "He was heading toward the train station."

The Vega twins and the Thea Sisters exchanged a meaningful look. They knew what they had to do: follow in the pawsteps of this **MYSTERIOUS** thief!

An Old Friendship

"Come on, we've got to get to the station before the thief ESCAPES!" Anita cried.

Joaquin, Nicky, Pam, and Colette joined her. Paulina and Violet decided to stay behind to see if they could uncover any CLUES.

Together, the two mouselets searched the *caseta* from floor to ceiling, but they didn't find **anything** helpful. So Violet and Paulina turned to Anita and Joaquin's parents and asked if they had noticed anything.

"Not me. I was playing my guitar the whole time. When I play, I CONCENTRATE only on the music," said Javier. He sounded upset.

"I noticed a rodent with a hat, too," Mama Lucia said. "He seemed familiar, but I can't quite put my paw on WHY. . . ."

"Now that you squeak it, he did seem **Familiar**. . . ." Vanessa murmured. "But I can't get a clear picture of him in my mind."

"We can help with that!" Violet exclaimed. "Paulina, do you have your MousePad with you?"

"Of course," her friend replied, **PULLING** out her tablet computer. "What do you have in mind?"

"Open the Identikit app! We'll create a sketch of the **THIEF**," Violet suggested.

With help from Vanessa, José, and Mama Lucia, Paulina **reconstructed** the thief's looks.

"No, his snout was a bit longer. . . ."

"And his cheekbones a little higher . . ."

"His **SNOUT** was hidden by his hat, but his eyes seemed **DARKER** to me. . . ."

After a few minutes, the mouselets found

themselves staring into the snout of a young, MYSTERIOUS-LOOKING rodent.

"That's . . . that's Carlos!" Julieta cried.

"You're right! IT'S HIM!" Mama Lucia added.

"Who are you squeaking about?" Paulina asked.

"He's an old friend of Julieta's, a great GUITAR player. They performed together years ago," Vanessa explained. "When they appeared onstage TOGETHER, their harmony took your breath away. The connection between

. . . a longer snout . . .

. . . higher cheekbones . . .

. . . that's Carlos!

music and dance was **PERFECT**!"

"Yes . . . what a shame they didn't last longer!" Mama Lucia said *SADLY*.

"What do you mean?" Violet asked curiously.

"Carlos disappeared just a few hours before the performance that would have secured them a CONTRACT with the

Julieta and Carlos performing together

most important theater in the city," Vanessa explained.

"**But why?**" asked Violet.

"I don't know why," Julieta *SIGHED*. "Carlos just vanished without a word. I haven't seen him since then."

"That's incredible! But why would he come back now?" Paulina asked.

"I have no idea. And I don't understand WHY he would take my fan, either."

Vanessa shook her snout. "I don't believe that he would really have **stolen** it. . . ."

"It's been years since we've heard anything about him," Julieta said sadly. "We have no way of knowing if he's still the **kind** rodent he once was, or if he's changed."

"We'll **find** him soon," Paulina declared. "The others are already on his trail. With a little bit of luck, they might have already tracked him down!"

THE CHASE!

Just then, Paulina got a **text message** from Nicky:

> ✉ **Nicky**
>
> We saw him get on a train for Granada. Meet us at the station. We're leaving!

"Granada . . . that's where Carlos is from," Julieta said. "He came to **Seville** to study music with a famouse guitarist."

"It's so strange," Violet reflected. "After YEARS without squeaking to you, this Carlos pops up out of nowhere. He takes your fan and then goes back to his **hometown**. What could he be thinking?"

"There's only one way to find out — we've got to **FOLLOW** him!" Paulina exclaimed.

"Yes, let's go!" Julieta said.

"My dear, you and Rodrigo have FOUR performances in the next two days," Mama Lucia interrupted. "Let Anita and Joaquin and the mouselets go without you. Together they'll solve this MYSTERY!"

Julieta sighed. "You're right. I can't cancel my shows. But I can help you with the search — I still have Carlos's address in Granada. I wrote to him there, but I never received a reply. . . ."

She pulled out an ADDRESS BOOK and gave

the information to Paulina.

"Before you leave, you should go back to the house," Mama Lucia said. "You can't **investigate** a mystery in flamenco dresses!"

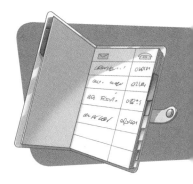

Violet and Paulina burst out **laughing**. They had been so focused on the theft, they'd completely forgotten how they were dressed.

"You're right, Mama Lucia," said Violet. "In these *gowns*, we'd stand out like bobcats in a bird preserve!"

Back at the Vega house, Violet and Paulina changed and filled their backpacks with fresh **clothes** for their friends. Mama Lucia packed them a lunch and a map of Granada. Then she drove them to the **TRAIN STATION**.

Anita, Joaquin, Colette, Nicky, and Pam were

anxiously waiting for them at the entrance.

"Flying fish sticks, **WHAT** took you so long!? Quick, the next train for Granada is about to leave!" Colette cried.

"We **DISCOVERED** something important! We'll **EXPLAIN** everything on the train," Violet said.

CLUE!

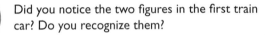

The seven friends scurried on board the train. They were in such a hurry, they didn't notice two sneaky SHADOWS spying on them from one of the train's windows. . . .

Did you notice the two figures in the first train car? Do you recognize them?

DESTINATION: GRANADA

After everyone had changed out of their *flamenco* costumes, Paulina and Violet told the others what they had discovered.

"I was little back then, but I remember Carlos! He and Aunt Julieta were INSEPARABLE. He was a very nice mouse," Anita commented.

"That's how I remember him, too!" Joaquin agreed. "He always took the time to play with us."

Colette **SMILED**. "Do you remember anything else about him?"

The siblings **Shook** their snouts.

"We'll just have to go to his house and hope to find him there. . . ." Pam said.

Violet studied the **map** of the city

carefully. When they arrived in Granada, she led them to Carlos's home without hesitation.

The city was beautiful, and the mouselets wished they had time to EXPLORE, but first they needed to find the fan. Julieta wouldn't have a moment's PEACE until it was BACK in her paws!

Granada

This Andalusian city is an important cultural center that's rich in architectural wonders. Its most striking spots are hidden in old neighborhoods such as the ALBAYZÍN, with its narrow streets, white houses, and ancient villas, and the SACROMONTE, which is built on the ruins of Roman catacombs. But the true jewel of Granada is the ALHAMBRA, a sprawling fortress built on a hillside overlooking the city.

GRANADA

Carlos lived in a **BIG** building with an interior courtyard. Colette, Nicky, Pam, Paulina, Violet, Anita, and Joaquin were looking for his NaMe on the buzzer when a deep squeak **surprised** them. "Do you need something?"

It was the building's superintendent. He was a stout rodent with a **LARGE** bunch of keys at his waist.

"We're looking for Carlos," Joaquin said. "We're Old friends of his."

"Ah, the musician!" the superintendent said. "He's not here. I saw him a little while ago, but he was in a **HURRY.**"

"Did you see which way he went, by any chance?" Anita asked.

"Oh, sure, I can tell you more than that. He said he was going to the **JEWELER** at the corner of San Nicolás Square. You can wait for him here. I don't think he'll be gone long —"

Before he could **FINISH**, Anita had thanked him, and the little group ran off. They scrambled through the streets of the Albayzín neighborhood, which was a JUMBLE

of picturesque white buildings.

"The square must be at the end of this street," said Violet, examining her **MAP**.

When they entered the square at last, the mouselets stopped and gazed in awe. On the hill in front of them was a truly breathtaking sight.

"That's the **ALHAMBRA**!" Joaquin said. "The **FORTRESS**

THE ALHAMBRA

Alhambra means "the red citadel" in Arabic. The name seems to come from the red clay used to build its walls.

The **Mexuar** is the oldest hall, where the council of ministers would meet.

The **Patio de los Arrayanes**, or Court of Myrtles, takes its name from the fragrant myrtle bushes that grow around a large pool.

The Alhambra is a walled city built on the side of a hill next to Granada. Construction began in 1238, during the reign of the founder of the Nasrid dynasty, Ibn el-Ahmar. As time passed, the structure grew until it became what it is today: an enchanting place, the pride of the city.

The architecture of the Alhambra was designed to achieve perfection in every detail. Every stone, inscription, and corner was placed with grace, harmony, and elegance.

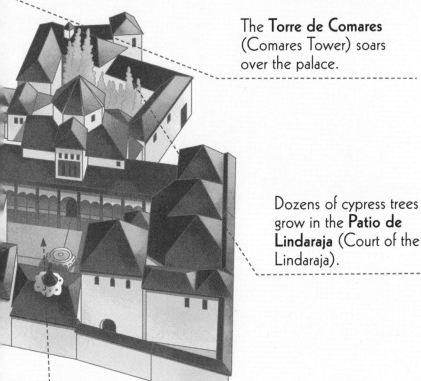

The **Torre de Comares** (Comares Tower) soars over the palace.

Dozens of cypress trees grow in the **Patio de Lindaraja** (Court of the Lindaraja).

The **Patio de los Leones** (Court of the Lions) is circled by 124 marble columns. In the center flows a fountain decorated with twelve lion statues.

was once home to the RULERS of the city."

"Mouselets, there's the jeweler!" Nicky exclaimed, pointing to a **small shop** a short distance away. "Quick, it's closing!"

But before the Thea Sisters and their friends could make a move, the shop owner lowered the SHUTTERS.

Everyone looked at one another. No one knew what to do next.

Then Anita exclaimed, "**OVER THERE!** It's Carlos!"

CARLOS'S TALE

Anita pointed to a rodent a few yards away. He had a **backpack** on his shoulders, and he was busy undoing a bike lock.

"Are you sure that's him?" Paulina asked.

"**DEFINITELY!**" Anita exclaimed.

As Colette, Nicky, Pam, Paulina, Violet, Anita, and Joaquin moved toward him, Carlos climbed on his bicycle and **PEDALED** out of the square. A moment later, he was zooming down an alley.

Quicker than a cat with a ball of yarn, the mouselets scurried after him. Soon, they were **BREATHLESS** trying to keep him in sight. That's when they heard a cry.

"Oh! Ouch!"

The mice turned and saw Colette on the

ground, *holding* her left leg.

Joaquin rushed over to her. "Are you hurt?" he asked, CONCERNED.

"No, it's just a cramp!" she replied, grimacing.

"Lean on me!" he said, helping her up.

"Oh no, we've lost sight of Carlos! MY BAD!" Colette apologized.

"Don't worry," Anita reassured her. "We'll try his house again."

The group began retracing their steps. Steadily, they drew closer to Carlos's building. After a few minutes, Paulina exclaimed, "Hey, look!"

Locked to a pole was a bicycle identical to the one that Carlos had been riding!

A **MOMENT** later, the rodent emerged from a travel agency. This time, the mouselets were determined not to let him **escape**. They immediately surrounded him.

"Hey, you're . . . you're . . . Anita and Joaquin!" he exclaimed, AMAZED. "What are you doing here?"

"Actually, that's what we've been planning to ask you," Anita replied coldly.

"Me?" he started, **surprised**, "I'm going back home to —"

"To hide the fan that you **STOLE** from our aunt?" Joaquin accused him.

"Wait, **WHAT**? No, there's been a misunderstanding!" *exclaimed* Carlos, blushing **REDDER** than a tomato. "It's true, I took Julieta's fan, but I just wanted to surprise her. . . . I'll show you."

Carlos took his **BACKPACK** off his

shoulders and opened it. "Here, **LOOK**. Wait . . . no, this can't be right!" he cried. "The fan is **GONE**!"

"What did you say?" Nicky asked.

"I put it in here a **MOMENT** ago. . . . Someone must have **STOLEN** it!"

"Are you telling us that someone stole the **fan** that you stole from Julieta?" asked Violet, staring him down.

"That's not how it was!" Carlos said firmly. "I didn't steal the fan, I just . . . **borrowed** it." He **SANK** down on a bench and put his snout in his paws. "You see, I haven't seen your aunt since I left Seville, but I've never stopped **thinking** about her." Carlos's squeak was both sweet and sad.

Who stole the fan from Carlos's backpack? Why?

"But why did you leave?" Anita asked.

"I never had Julieta's **CONFIDENCE** onstage. She was always so brave, so **FEARLESS** in front of an audience. I was always terrified of making a mistake and RUINING our shows!"

"Stage fright is totally normal," Anita said. "It happens to us, too, when we dance!"

"You just need to **be brave** and face your fears," Joaquin agreed.

"I know that now, but back then, I was a SCAREDY-MOUSE. I let my stage fright get the better of me," Carlos said. "I didn't even have the courage to tell Julieta I hadn't written a song for our PERFORMANCE!"

"So why come back now?" Joaquin asked.

"Because now my song is ready. And I want to SHOW Julieta that I'm worthy of accompanying the greatest dancer in all of Spain!"

"But what about the FAN?" Colette asked.

NEW CLUES!

"It was supposed to be a surprise for Julieta," Carlos explained. "I wanted to talk to her last night. I was going to ask her FORGIVENESS — and confess my love for her. But when I saw her gorgeous fan, I had an idea. . . ."

"What idea?" Violet asked.

"I wanted to INSCRIBE the final verse

of the song I wrote for her on the handle. I'd bring it to my trusty jeweler, here in Granada. He could do it right away, and I didn't think she'd miss the fan. I never meant to make such a mess of things!"

"Carlos, I don't think you understand how

precious that fan is to our FAMILY. It belonged to **Rosita**. It was part of our inheritance," Anita explained.

"What?! If I had known that, I would never have taken it!" Carlos cried.

"What matters now is that we find it," Joaquin said. "Any idea who might have STOLEN it from you?"

"Let me think for a minute," Carlos replied. "I put it in my backpack when I went into the travel agency to BUY a train ticket for Seville. . . ."

"Did you meet anyone?" Violet asked him.

"No . . . Wait a sec, yes, I did," Carlos said. "A tourist stopped me to ask for directions to the **ALHAMBRA**. Do you think she might have stolen it?"

"It's possible!" Anita declared. "Tell us EXACTLY what happened."

"It was a young mouselet. She came up behind me and asked for directions. I turned to SHOW her which street to take, but when I turned around again, she had DISAPPEARED!"

"That seems SUSPICIOUS," Colette murmured.

Who is the mysterious mouselet who stopped Carlos?

CLUE!

"After the mouselet disappeared, I found this piece of **PAPER** on the ground," Carlos said. "I was going to throw it away, but . . ."

"Read it to us," Anita said.

Plaza Santa Teresa – Córdoba

Trains Seville – Granada:
9:10 – 10:10 – 11:10
Trains Granada – Córdoba:
1:00 – 1:30 – 2:00

"Plaza Santa Teresa . . . that **ADDRESS** sounds familiar," Joaquin murmured.

"Of course it's familiar!" Anita exclaimed.

The Thea Sisters were surprised. "Do you **kn0w** someone who lives there?" Violet asked.

"Yes, that's the address for Rosita's house," Anita explained.

"You're a **GENIUS**, sis! How could I have forgotten?" Joaquin cried.

"These are the train schedules for **Seville**, *Granada*, and CÓRDOBA," Carlos observed. "Something smells funnier than feta cheese. That tourist didn't say anything about Córdoba. She asked me for directions to the **ALHAMBRA!**"

"Maybe that was just an excuse to distract you and take the fan," Paulina suggested.

"Hmm . . ." Violet said. "It looks like there's another train trip in our future."

Pam nodded. "Let's go, mouselets! Córdoba is calling!"

"I'll come with you," offered Carlos.

"Actually, we have another job for you," Joaquin said. "Someone needs to go back to

Seville to explain things to Julieta. Will you go?"

Carlos nodded. "Of course. But stay in touch and **be careful**!"

WHAT DO YOU THINK IS GOING ON? LET'S REVIEW THE CLUES!

- The stolen fan is an important Vega family heirloom. It belonged to Joaquin and Anita's ancestor Rosita.

- Carlos took the fan to create a surprise for Julieta. He didn't realize that it was Rosita's fan.

- The only rodent he ran into was a mysterious tourist. Could she be the one who took the fan?

- The tourist asked for information about the Alhambra, but she dropped the schedule for trains to Córdoba.

A REVEALING
RATNAP!

Half an hour later, the Thea Sisters, Joaquin, and Anita were on board a train, this time bound for Córdoba. Pam **threw** herself onto a seat in their compartment. "Back on the **TRAIN** again! By tonight we'll have seen ALL of Spain through this window."

"And without a *wink* of sleep," murmured Violet. Her eyelids were starting to droop. A moment later, she had drifted off, HUGGING her backpack tight to her chest.

"Whoa, what a sleepysnout!" Anita exclaimed. "Should we wake her?"

"No, no, no, no! Don't even think about it!" Colette said, grabbing her friend's paw. "Violet gets **grouchier** than a

groundhog if she doesn't get her z's. . . ."

"And you *don't* want to be the one to wake her," Paulina added, giggling.

"That's too bad. We could use her help reviewing the clues," Anita said.

"Let's start WITHOUT her," Joaquin suggested. "Okay, so Carlos took the fan from Julieta's purse, but then someone took it from him!"

"Probably someone who followed him from Seville . . ." Nicky observed.

". . . and who knew it wasn't just any fan!" Colette concluded.

"It's Rosita's fan, and the thief seems to be headed for her HOUSE," Anita added. "She must be looking for something . . . but what?"

"THE TREASURE!"

Violet exclaimed, waking suddenly.

Her friends stared at her in **SURPRISE**.

"What treasure?!" Pam asked.

"You're not going to believe this, but I just dreamed about Rosita, who told me to pay attention to her **TREASURE**," Violet said.

"You mean the song?" Joaquin asked.

"Yes, but I have a feeling it's more than that. Can you ask Julieta to send us a few **pictures** of Rosita and her house?"

"Of course, but why?" asked Anita.

"I have an **idea**, but I need to make sure I'm not leading us on a wild-cat chase!"

A few moments later, Julieta **texted** Anita scans of old photographs of Rosita. The first showed her during a PERFORMANCE. It looked like a snapshot from an audience member. The second was a portrait of the **DANCER** in a classic pose, wearing a *gorgeous* red dance costume and with a proud look on her snout.

In the third, a much younger Rosita sat on a chair in her living room in the house in *Granada.* She was *SMILING* at the photographer.

"There!" Violet exclaimed, pointing at a detail in the LAST photo. "That's it! Mouselets . . . and Joaquin . . . I think my unconscious is onto something!"

THE SECRET
OF THE SONG

The friends **LOOKED** at Violet in amazement.

"Do you think Vi is squeaking in her sleep?" Pam whispered in Nicky's ear, which made her friend **giggle**.

But the confident voice of their friend silenced them. "Now we could use **a little help** from Rodrigo. Could you call him?"

"Of course . . ." Joaquin replied, dialing his brother's **NUMBER**.

"Bro, we need your help!" he said, passing the phone to Violet.

She made a strange request: "Could you sing Rosita's **song** for us?"

"You mean right now? On the phone?" Rodrigo replied hesitantly. Colette, Nicky,

Pam, Paulina, Anita, and Joaquin looked at one another, **perplexed**.

"Yes, please. It's very important!"

Rodrigo cleared his throat. Violet put him on **SQUEAKERPHONE**, and he began to sing.

"My treasure is hidden
In a garden of rose.
The way to its heart
Is something no one knows."

"**STOP RIGHT THERE!**" Violet said, interrupting him. "Did you hear that? A garden of r0se! Don't you get it? The answer is right in front of us!"

Pam looked around, CONFUSED. "Uh, all I see is an old train compartment. . . . There's no **TRACE** of roses here!"

It was Nicky's turn to whisper in her friend's ear: "Don't argue with her! Maybe she just needs more time for her ratnap. . . ."

Violet rolled her eyes. "I heard that! I'm wide-**AWAKE**. Don't you understand **WHAT** I'm suggesting? The TREASURE in the song really does exist, and Rosita is telling us how to FIND it!"

"You're saying there really is a rose garden?" Colette asked.

"Yes . . . no! It's not a real garden. **LOOK** at this last **picture**. Behind Rosita, there's a wooden **sideboard** with a very particular carving. . . ."

"**Roses!**" Anita exclaimed.

"Exactly! The treasure is in its heart . . . that is, in the **sideboard**!" Violet exclaimed.

Joaquin was skeptical. "But how do you know that's **TRUE**? It might just be a **coincidence**!"

Violet smiled. "Maybe . . . but who knows? Rodrigo, please, could you continue with the SONG?"

Rodrigo's deep squeak echoed through the compartment once more.

"My treasure is known only to me.
It can never be taken apart.
Its key commands the wind,
And it stays always near my heart."

"Of course! She's talking about her **fan**!" Anita exclaimed. "The fan commands the wind. And Rosita always kept it **CLOSE** to her heart!"

"But what does that mean?" Pam asked.

"There must be a hiding place inside the **sideboard**, and the key to opening it is the fan," Violet explained.

"The key? That's interesting . . . I've always wondered why the **HANDLE** has such a strange shape. It's very **different** from most traditional fans," Anita said.

"That explains why it was stolen!" her brother said. "The thief understood that the SONG was a map to find the treasure!"

"So what do you think the TREASURE is?" Nicky asked.

"Let's listen to the end of the song. I bet it will give us more CLUES!" Paulina suggested.

Rodrigo cleared his throat and sang.

"My treasure remains hidden.
It does not easily come out.
It waits for the brightest star
To shine down on my snout.

"Where are you, my treasure?
Far and wide will I roam,
Though the place where I'll find you
Is close to my home."

When Rodrigo stopped **SINGING**, the compartment was so quiet, you could hear a cheese slice drop. The mouselets looked at one another, their minds racing.

Finally, Pam broke the silence. "**SISTERS**, I have to admit something. I'm more lost than a rat in a maze!"

"Me, too!" Violet confessed **unhappily**.

AT ROSITA'S HOUSE

When the Thea Sisters, Anita, and Joaquin got off the **TRAIN** at Córdoba, the sky was bright pink, and the sun had already **sunk** behind the hills.

Anita quickly hailed two **taxis**. "It's a bit of a hike from here," she said.

She **directed** the drivers to Plaza Santa Teresa. "That's where the museum is," she explained.

"Great!" Pamela replied. "Um . . . what **MUSEUM** are you talking about? We're here to go to Rosita's house, not to go sightseeing. . . ."

Joaquin laughed. "So sorry, we should have explained! Rosita's house has been turned into a **MUSEUM**."

"That's right," Anita said. "Every room has been **preserved** just as it was back then, and there are clothes, **GUITARS**, and

Córdoba

You can see the ancient history of Córdoba in what remains of its ancient walls, bridges, towers, and palaces. This walled city once served as both the Roman and Moorish capital of Spain.

Madrid

Seville

Granada

ANDALUSIA

CÓRDOBA

Of all Córdoba's monuments, the splendid MEZQUITA, or mosque, stands out. It has more than 850 columns made of jasper, onyx, marble, and granite.

Córdoba is famous for its craftsmen creating high-quality jewelry, pottery, and fans!

PHOTOGRAPHS on display. There's even a section about the history of *flamenco*."

The taxis rushed through the city streets and crossed the RIVER Guadalquivir. Its calm water shimmered below the city lights, and the **breeze** blowing into the car windows carried the sweet scent of flowers.

"When we've solved the mystery of the fan, Anita and I would love to take you all on a TOUR of the city of our ancestors," Joaquin said.

"That would be lovely. It's so beautiful," Colette murmured, admiring a majestic bridge in the distance.

The taxis stopped in front of an ancient building. The friends thanked the drivers and hurried to the museum's entrance.

"It's closed!" Pam exclaimed, disappointed.

"Unfortunately, it doesn't reopen until

tomorrow morning," Violet said, reading the hours posted on the **locked** door.

"So now what do we do?" Anita asked, worried. "We can't wait till tomorrow!"

"**WAIT, WAIT, WAIT** . . . look up there!" Colette exclaimed, pointing to a small balcony on the second floor. Dim light **FILTERED** out of the window.

"There's a light on. There must be someone inside. Let's go **UP** there!" Nicky suggested.

"But how?" asked Anita.

Paulina noticed that one of the glass doors to the balcony was slightly open, and she pointed to a few large boxes that were **stacked** up on the sidewalk. "We can make a pile out of those!"

The **mouselets** quickly hoisted themselves up onto the balcony, one after the other.

YOU?!

All the mouselets and their friends had to do was push open the window, which someone had already FORCED open. Colette, Nicky, Pam, Paulina, Violet, Joaquin, and Anita found themselves in a dark room that smelled of roses.

"Be careful where you put your . . ."

BAM!

"**YEE-OUCH!**" Pam cried, rubbing her head.

Paulina **TURNED** on her MousePhone. Its light shone onto the columns of a four-poster bed. Pam had walked right into it.

"We're in Rosita's bedroom,"

Anita said. "**FOLLOW** me. The **living room** is through there!"

Just then, they heard the sound of an object falling. Someone was **SQUEAKING** softly.

"The thieves! This is our chance to see who they are," said Nicky, moving toward the **noise**.

"Wait!" Paulina stopped her. "Let's be ready to call the **POLICE** in case we need them."

As the seven friends entered the living room, they saw two **figures** with their backs turned. They were fiddling with a sideboard decorated with **carved** roses.

"Stop right there! We've caught you!" Joaquin shouted.

The two **mysterious** thieves turned around. "**YOU?!**" everyone gasped.

Who do you think the mysterious thieves are?

THE SECRET DRAWER

Lola and Pedro Navarro looked every bit as SURPRISED as the Thea Sisters and their friends!

"Slimy Swiss cheese, I should have known the Navarro family was behind this!" Joaquin hissed, approaching the twins. "You stole Aunt Julieta's fan!"

"Of course!" Violet said. "You were there at Rodrigo's performance, and you heard Rosita's SONG!"

Pedro and Lola were forced to confess. "Yes, we heard the song. But it was what Julieta said about Rosita's TREASURE that made us realize it was more than a simple melody — it was also a CLUE," Pedro replied.

Lola sounded **ANGRY**. "We realized what it meant right away, unlike you Vegas. You had the SONG in your paws all along, and you **NEVER** took the time to understand it!"

"I can't believe you're pointing a paw at us!" Anita **exclaimed**. "You should have come to us to talk about the **treasure** instead of stealing the fan!"

"Why would we do that? The treasure belongs to **US** just as much as you. It's all about who finds it first!" Pedro cried.

"But you **only** found it because you **STOLE** our aunt's fan!" Joaquin protested.

Pedro lowered his eyes. "Well, none of that matters now, because we haven't found any **treasure**!"

Violet **stepped** toward the sideboard. "What? The rose **garden** is here, and you have the key — that is, the **fan**. It didn't work?"

"Yes, it worked," Lola replied. "When we inserted the handle into the hole in the central **rose**, it unsnapped the lock. But . . ."

"But what?" Anita asked.

"Look for yourselves!" Pedro sighed.

Violet examined the sideboard. A simple **panel** hid a secret drawer, which was

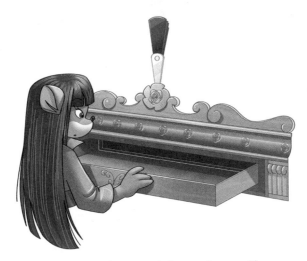

empty. "There's nothing there!"

"Exactly," Pedro said. "Rosita's **TREASURE** doesn't exist."

"Maybe someone else already **took** it!" Lola snapped.

"I don't think that's what happened," murmured Colette, who had been eyeing Lola for a few **moments**.

"What do you mean?" Lola asked **shortly**.

"Your fur-do —"

"Um, Colette . . . ?" Nicky **INTERRUPTED**. "This isn't exactly the best time to discuss the latest **furstyles**!"

CLUE!

"Oh, I know, I know!" Colette said, waving a paw. "There's a time and a place for my passion for fashion. It's just that I think the **SOLUTION** to this puzzle is right in Lola's fur!"

 What is it about Lola's fur-do that Colette finds so distracting?

THE BRIGHTEST STAR

BEWILDERED, Lola stared at Colette. "But . . . there's nothing in my fur. I don't know what you're talking about!"

"Colette, you're brainier than a bookmouse!" Violet exclaimed. "Lola's comb looks just like the one we **SAW** in Rosita's photo."

"It doesn't just *look* like it, it's the exact same one! It's a **FAMILY** heirloom. But I don't understand why that matters. . . ." Anita said.

"Just think about the third verse of the SONG!" said Colette. "It's about a **BRIGHT STAR** that illuminates Rosita's snout. And that comb is in the shape of a star!"

"Are you saying that the comb is a KEY, too?" Paulina asked.

"If it is, there must be another LOCK!" Joaquin guessed. He ran his paw over the insides of the drawer. "I feel something here!"

Colette joined him. They spotted three small holes at the back of the drawer. When Lola took the comb from her fur, they could see that the little holes were exactly the same size as the three teeth of the comb.

Gently, Lola inserted the comb into the holes, and they heard a soft *click*. The bottom of the drawer opened, revealing a **secret compartment**.

"The treasure!" Colette exclaimed, pulling out a wooden box.

"Give it to me!" Pedro exclaimed, lunging for the box.

But Joaquin stopped him. "We'll open it

TOGETHER. Rosita would have wanted it that way."

The rodents sat down in a CIRCLE on the living room floor. Colette took the precious box and opened it slowly. Inside were a bundle of yellowed papers covered in elegant script, along with a sealed envelope.

Colette LOOKED at the papers, not understanding what they could be, and passed them to her friends.

"They're SONGS!" Pedro exclaimed. "They're signed by Rosita, but I don't recognize them. . . ."

"You're right," Anita confirmed. "I think they're unpublished!"

"This truly is a treasure!" Joaquin breathed.

Lola took the envelope. *"To Blanca and Beatriz, my LOVELY daughters,"* she read. She opened it carefully.

My dear daughters,

 If you are reading these words, it means that my fondest wish has come true. My heart has suffered every day that you two have argued.

 That's why I decided to hide a part of your inheritance in a place that needs two keys — the fan that you have, Blanca, and the comb that I left to you, Beatriz. To find my treasure, you would need to work together.

 This is a collection of songs that I composed after I left the stage. I wanted to express my deepest feelings, and to preserve them for those who would understand them. No one appreciates the spirit of flamenco better than you two.

 Please, for my sake, you must abandon the rivalry that divides you. Listen to your hearts. Only then can you continue to give life to my greatest passion.

      Your loving mama,
      Rosita

A NEW ALLIANCE

Lola put the LETTER back in the envelope. Then she looked up at her brother with shining eyes.

"So . . ." Pam said, breaking the silence, "this is all part of Rosita's **PLAN**!"

"Yes, she wanted to make peace between her daughters and **REUNITE** her family," Paulina added.

"But it didn't work," Pedro murmured. "Blanca and Beatriz never got over their grudges."

"They didn't, but we can!" Anita exclaimed.

Everyone turned to gaze at her. Anita had a DETERMINED look on her snout.

"Think about it!" she continued. "The **rivalry** between the Vegas and the Navarros goes back a long time, but what started it? A simple **ARGUMENT** between two sisters! Does **ANYONE** even know what it was about?"

Pedro and Lola exchanged a look: It was hard to admit, but Anita was **RIGHT**!

"There's never been a real reason for us to *fight*...." Lola reflected.

"Why should we argue? We don't **EVEN** know each other!" Anita agreed. She smiled shyly at her cousin.

"The *fighting* between our families has lasted for many years," Pedro chimed in. "We've been sworn **enemies** since we were mouselings!"

"It's true. We've always considered you and

your school our **BIGGEST** rivals," Joaquin added.

Pedro shook his snout. "That can't be. Our school is about to close!"

The Vega twins were stunned. "Is the situation really that **SERIOUS**?" Anita asked.

"Yes," Lola confirmed. "That's why we did everything we could to get the TREASURE. We hoped that it would help us save the school, but now . . ."

Pedro shook his head sadly. He turned to his sister. "We just have to accept the fact that our school's days are numbered."

Joaquin stood UP and took his cousin's paw. "It doesn't have to be that way. Pedro, Lola, it's **up to us** to change things. We can't change the PAST, but we can choose what will happen in the future!" he DECLARED.

Pedro looked amazed. "But how?"

Anita understood her brother perfectly. "It's simple. We just need to follow Rosita's advice: *We'll listen to our hearts!*"

"My heart tells me that we four mice have a **LOT** in common," Joaquin added. "We should join forces . . . and SCHOOLS!"

"What? Do you mean that the Vegas and

the Navarros could found a single, large *flamenco* school?!" Lola asked.

"That's a **MARVEMOUSE** idea!" Colette exclaimed, jumping to her paws. The other THEA SISTERS nodded in agreement.

"Do you think that's possible, Joaquin?" Pedro asked.

"Of course!" his cousin replied. "We can create a new repertoire with the SONGS we discovered today. They belong **equally** to the Vegas and the Navarros."

"At last, we understand what Rosita's true TREASURE is!" Colette cried.

"Yes, her ENCHANTING songs!" Anita exclaimed.

Colette shook her snout. "Not just that. There's something even **more important**. Rosita wanted her daughters to know that it's better to be TOGETHER, because

T°GETHER we are stronger!"

Nicky, Pamela, Paulina, and Violet nodded.

"FRIENDS TOGETHER, MICE FOREVER!"

RETURN TO SEVILLE

As Colette, Nicky, Pam, Paulina, Violet, Anita, Joaquin, Lola, and Pedro left the museum, they realized **night** had fallen.

"Now what? Should we catch a train back to **Seville**?" Paulina asked.

"Crusty carburetors! If you want me to get on another *train* today, you'll have to drag me by the tail!" Pam cried.

Anita laughed. "Don't worry, I asked Rodrigo and Aunt Julieta to come pick us up in our van. They won't be **LONG**."

"Yay! In that case, why don't we stop for a **SNACK**?" Pam asked. "I don't know about you mice, but I'm hungrier than a rodent on a MouseFast diet."

"There's a **RESTAURANT** over there," Paulina

said, pointing to a corner of the square.

Sure enough, there was a little café labeled **CASA JULIO**. A waiter with a bushy **mustache** invited the rodents to sit down at an outdoor table.

"**MOUSELETS**, do you trust us? If you do, we'll order all the best *Spanish*

specialties for you!" Pedro said.

The Thea Sisters *gladly* agreed. Ten minutes later, the waiter who had greeted them placed a **LARGE** pot full of rice and seafood on the table in front of them.

"Mmm . . . that 𝕊𝕞𝕖𝕝𝕝𝕤 fabumouse!" Colette exclaimed.

PaeLLa

Paella is a traditional dish originally from Valencia. It's made of saffron-flavored rice, vegetables, meat, and seafood. Paella started as a peasant's dish, made from leftovers, but quickly became a beloved gourmet recipe! It is usually cooked and served in an iron pot.

"It's delicious!" Pam echoed. She was so hungry, she dug her fork right into the **POT**.

"What is it?" Violet asked.

"**PaeLLa!** It's my favorite dish," Pedro replied.

The next fifteen minutes were filled with munching, CRUNCHING, and chatting. As the mice were finishing up their meal, Anita's phone rang.

"It's Auntie Julieta. She and Rodrigo are **here**," Anita said.

Everyone turned and recognized the Vega

family's **VAN**. Julieta and Rodrigo were **waving** from the front seat.

The group joined them right away. Julieta greeted her niece and nephew and the **THEA SISTERS joyfully**, but her smile disappeared when she saw Rosita's fan in Lola's paws.

"But that's . . . that's **my** fan!" Julieta cried.

Rodrigo stiffened, too. "Then *you* must have **taken** it! But how . . . ?"

Joaquin stepped forward. "Please, let us explain. We have a great **IDEA** to share with you. We'll tell you all about it on the way home."

MEETING AT MIDNIGHT

On the ride back to Seville, the young rodents told Julieta and Rodrigo everything. As soon as they heard about Rosita's letter, they agreed to the plan.

Once they were back in Seville, the Vegas and the Navarros split up to put that plan into action!

"Let's meet at midnight at the *feria*!" Lola exclaimed. Then she and her brother SQUEEZED down a narrow street.

"Those two are **sweeter** than cheese dumplings with syrup on top. If only we'd known sooner!" Rodrigo said.

"Yes, I'm so happy to have found two new friends," Anita said. "Mouselets, why don't you go GET READY? Joaquin and I will LOOK for our parents."

The Thea Sisters felt like they were going back in time to the day before.

"Can you believe we came to Seville just a day ago?" Violet mused. "We've done so much, it'll take HOURS to tell Thea about it!"

"It certainly wasn't the relaxing  vacation we were hoping for," said Nicky, winking at her friends.

"Maybe not," Colette said. "But it was definitely worth it to spend time with our friends."

When everyone was dressed for flamenco, they scampered into the heart of the *feria*. There was a fireworks display planned for midnight.

"I'm so happy that you found the FAN!" Mama Lucia said once they were all together again. "But I still don't understand how exactly you did it. . . ."

"You'll find out SOON, Mama," Anita said.

Inside the *caseta*, the VEGAS and the mouselets were **reunited** with the Navarros: Pedro and Lola, plus their parents, Luis and Maria. There was an ICY moment when Mama Lucia and Papa Javier spotted them. But the tension melted faster than fondue in a pot when their sons and daughters rushed to hug one another.

"WHAT in the name of cheese is going on?" Maria exclaimed.

"Mama, Papa, in Córdoba we found not just the fan, but also Rosita's TRUE treasure. Look!" said Joaquin, holding up the bundle of SONGS.

"What's that?" the parents all asked at once.

"They're **unpublished** songs," Lola explained. "Rosita left them to us. . . ."

"To *all* of us?" her mother cried.

"Yes, Mama," Pedro said. "The Vegas and the Navarros have been **divided** for too long, and none of us even know why. It's time for us to become one **family** again —"

"Which is why we've decided that we should **join** forces and create a single flamenco school!" Lola finished.

The young rodents' **enthusiasm** was so unexpected and overwhelming that their parents couldn't help agreeing.

"It's true! Now is the time for friendship!"

At that moment, fireworks **EXPLODED** above their heads, filling the Seville sky with a thousand sparks of color.

DREAM WITH ME

Julieta looked on with a joyful **HEART** as her family members **hugged** one another. Suddenly, she heard a **deep** squeak saying her name. She didn't need to turn around to know who it was: Carlos, her old *friend*.

"Julieta . . . I'm back," he began. "Before you say anything, I'd like to explain that I **left** because I didn't have enough courage. I didn't have the courage to follow our **DREAMS**. But today I am here, and if you would like, we can begin our dreams together again!" He pawed her a bunch of **red roses**.

Then he pulled a folded piece of paper out of his pocket. "I composed this song for you. There's nothing I want more in the world

than to see you *twirling* to its notes! Would you do me the honor?"

Confused, Julieta clutched the roses to her chest. This rodent had broken her heart when he **FLED**. And now, after years, he had reappeared out of nowhere. *How could she trust him?*

Without another squeak, Carlos picked up his guitar and played a *sweet* chord.

"Carlos . . . you never wanted to sing because you were so shy!" Julieta murmured to herself. "I never knew that. . . ."

Then, his squeak full of emotion, Carlos began a **Heartfelt** song:

"My dearest love,
My greatest mistake was leaving you.
But now I have learned,
I have grown,
And I have found the courage

To follow my dreams.
So I ask you:
Will you dream with me?"

Julieta's eyes were SHINING with tears. Without thinking, she pawed the roses to Paulina and took Carlos's paws. "I'm ready to start **dreaming** with you!" she murmured.

"AT LAST, Julieta and Carlos are reunited, too!" Pam said.

"True love never **disappears** . . . and it conquers every obstacle!" Colette added.

Just then, Joaquin offered her his paw. "Colette, would you give me the honor of a **dance**?"

Under the sparkling lights of the city festival, the two young rodents leaped onstage and began to dance the *flamenco*.

"What a marvemouse night . . ." Nicky whispered.

Paulina smiled and sniffed the **roses** that she still clutched in her paws. "A sweet night with sweet friends!"

THEY WERE MORE THAN FRIENDS. THEY WERE SISTERS!

Thea Sisters

Want to read the next adventure
of the Thea Sisters?
I can't wait to tell you all about it!

THEA STILTON AND THE JOURNEY TO THE LION'S DEN

The Thea Sisters are in Kenya on a photo safari! The mouselets love exploring the magnificent landscape and learning about the animals on the reserve they're visiting. A lion cub has just been born — but while they're there, he's kidnapped! It's up to the Thea Sisters to rescue him in an adventure across the savanna.

Don't miss any of my fabumouse adventures!

Thea Stilton and the Dragon's Code

Thea Stilton and the Mountain of Fire

Thea Stilton and the Ghost of the Shipwreck

Thea Stilton and the Secret City

Thea Stilton and the Mystery in Paris

Thea Stilton and the Cherry Blossom Adventure

Thea Stilton and the Star Castaways

Thea Stilton: Big Trouble in the Big Apple

Thea Stilton and the Ice Treasure

Thea Stilton and the Secret of the Old Castle

Thea Stilton and the Blue Scarab Hunt

Thea Stilton and the Prince's Emerald

Thea Stilton and the Mystery on the Orient Express

Thea Stilton and the Dancing Shadows

Thea Stilton and the Legend of the Fire Flowers

Thea Stilton and the Spanish Dance Mission

Check out these very special editions featuring me and the Thea Sisters!

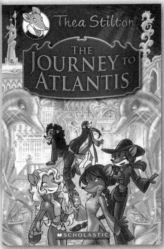

THE JOURNEY
TO ATLANTIS

THE SECRET OF
THE FAIRIES

Be sure to read these stories, too!

#1 Lost Treasure of the Emerald Eye

#2 The Curse of the Cheese Pyramid

#3 Cat and Mouse in a Haunted House

#4 I'm Too Fond of My Fur!

#5 Four Mice Deep in the Jungle

#6 Paws Off, Cheddarface!

#7 Red Pizzas for a Blue Count

#8 Attack of the Bandit Cats

#9 A Fabumouse Vacation for Geronimo

#10 All Because of a Cup of Coffee

#11 It's Halloween, You 'Fraidy Mouse!

#12 Merry Christmas, Geronimo!

#13 The Phantom of the Subway

#14 The Temple of the Ruby of Fire

#15 The Mona Mousa Code

#16 A Cheese-Colored Camper

#17 Watch Your Whiskers, Stilton!

#18 Shipwreck on the Pirate Islands

#19 My Name Is Stilton, Geronimo Stilton

#20 Surf's Up, Geronimo!

#21 The Wild, Wild West

#22 The Secret of Cacklefur Castle

A Christmas Tale

#23 Valentine's Day Disaster

#24 Field Trip to Niagara Falls

#25 The Search for Sunken Treasure

#26 The Mummy with No Name

#27 The Christmas Toy Factory

#28 Wedding Crasher

#29 Down and Out Down Under

#30 The Mouse Island Marathon

#31 The Mysterious Cheese Thief

Christmas Catastrophe

#32 Valley of the Giant Skeletons

#33 Geronimo and the Gold Medal Mystery

#34 Geronimo Stilton, Secret Agent

#35 A Very Merry Christmas

#36 Geronimo's Valentine

#37 The Race Across America

#38 A Fabumouse School Adventure

#39 Singing Sensation

#40 The Karate Mouse

#41 Mighty Mount Kilimanjaro

#42 The Peculiar Pumpkin Thief

#43 I'm Not a Supermouse!

#44 The Giant Diamond Robbery

#45 Save the White Whale!

#46 The Haunted Castle

#47 Run for the Hills, Geronimo!

#48 The Mystery in Venice

#49 The Way of the Samurai

#50 This Hotel Is Haunted!

#51 The Enormouse Pearl Heist

#52 Mouse in Space!

#53 Rumble in the Jungle

#54 Get into Gear Stilton

#55 The Golden Statue Plot

Be sure to check out my adventures in the Kingdom of Fantasy!

THE KINGDOM OF FANTASY

THE QUEST FOR PARADISE:
THE RETURN TO THE KINGDOM OF FANTASY

THE AMAZING VOYAGE:
THE THIRD ADVENTURE IN THE KINGDOM OF FANTASY

THE DRAGON PROPHECY:
THE FOURTH ADVENTURE IN THE KINGDOM OF FANTASY

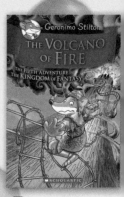

THE VOLCANO OF FIRE:
THE FIFTH ADVENTURE IN THE KINGDOM OF FANTASY

Meet
GERONIMO STILTONOOT

He is a cavemouse — Geronimo Stilton's ancient ancestor! He runs the stone newspaper in the prehistoric village of Old Mouse City. From dealing with dinosaurs to dodging meteorites, his life in the Stone Age is full of adventure!

Geronimo Stilton

CAVEMICE
THE STONE OF FIRE
SCHOLASTIC

Geronimo Stilton

CAVEMICE
WATCH YOUR TAIL!
SCHOLASTIC

Geronimo Stilton

CAVEMICE
HELP, I'M IN HOT LAVA!
SCHOLASTIC

THANKS FOR READING, AND GOOD-BYE UNTIL OUR NEXT ADVENTURE!

Thea Sisters